WHERE'S WALDO?
THE TREASURE HUNT
ACTIVITY BOOK
MARTIN HANDFORD

CANDLEWICK PRESS

W9-AUD-296

HI THERE, WALDO FANS!

I'M SETTING OFF ON AN ALMIGHTY ADVENTURE! YOU CAN COME TOO! ALL YOU HAVE TO DO IS PLAY THE PUZZLING PUZZLES USING YOUR BRAIN POWER AND A PEN OR PENCIL IN EACH PLACE WE TRAVEL TO. FIRST WE'LL JET OFF INTO OUTER SPACE, THEN WE'LL TAKE FLIGHT IN THE SKY, NEXT WE'LL HIKE OVER AND UNDER ANCIENT LANDS, AND FINALLY WE'LL SET SAIL OUT TO SEA. WOW! INCREDIBLE!

THAT'S NOT ALL! I'M ON THE LOOKOUT FOR FOUR TREMENDOUS TREASURES. CAN YOU HELP ME FIND ONE IN EACH PLACE WE JOURNEY TO?

STAR   FEATHER   GEM   SHELL

BY THE WAY, WE'RE NOT TRAVELING ON OUR OWN. WHEREVER WE GO, MY TRUSTY FRIENDS WENDA, WOOF, WIZARD WHITEBEARD, AND ODLAW GO TOO. SEARCH FOR OUR PRECIOUS POSSESSIONS IN EACH DESTINATION!

WALDO'S KEY   WOOF'S BONE   WENDA'S CAMERA   WIZARD WHITEBEARD'S SCROLL   ODLAW'S BINOCULARS

HAVE FANTASTIC FUN!

Waldo

Journey into outer space!

3, 2, 1 . . .
BLAST OFF WITH ME,
EARTH-DWELLERS, INTO
THE DEEPEST, DARKEST
DEPTHS OF SPACE. WE'LL
VISIT PUZZLING PLANETS,
PLAY GRAVITY-BENDING
GAMES, AND FIND ANSWERS
TO COSMIC CONUNDRUMS
AS WE GO. ALSO HELP ME
FIND THIS SUPER SPECIAL
SHINING STAR! IT'S
OUT OF THIS WORLD!

STAR

SPACE MAIL

Whoops! What an intergalactic mailroom mix-up!
Match each message to a stamp to find out
who did (and who didn't) send postcards.

TODAY I MET WOOF AND WENDA WAITING WITH ALIENS AT A SPACESHIP STOP. ONE OF THE ALIENS WAS WEARING A RED-POM-POM HAT—JUST LIKE MINE! WOW! WISH YOU WERE HERE!

WALDO-WATCHERS
WANDERING ABOUT,
PLANET EARTH,
THE UNIVERSE

Zip-zap-swoosh-boing! I cast a magic spell to make a rocket! Can you believe my beard got caught in its antenna and I was carried light-years away?

Waldo

Walking Here and There,

With a Walking Stick,

Wherever You Are

I'M FEELING
BLUE TODAY,
AND NOT JUST IN
COLOR. MY BROTHER (HE
STICKS HIS TONGUE
OUT A LOT!) WON'T TAKE
ME TO HIS SPACEBALL
MATCH ON PLANET
ZOG. CAN YOU MAKE IT
HAPPEN?

MAKE A WISH COME
TRUE INC.

LUCKY LETTERBOX,

SHOOTING STAR CITY

I SNOOZED IN THE SOLAR
HAMMOCK YOU SENT ME
AND FLOATED TOO CLOSE
TO THE SUN. I'M NOT
ORANGE ANYMORE AND MY
THREE EYES ARE SORE!
OUCH!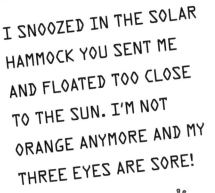

MOM

RED STAR STREET,

NEAR THE BLACK HOLE,

BESIDE PLANET WHOOPSY

RIDDLE ME THIS,
RIDDLE ME THAT,

I'M SNEAKING ABOUT LIKE
A BLACK CYBER CAT.

I HAVE SUNGLASSES
AND A MUSTACHE FOR
MY DISGUISE.

TRY TO TRACK DOWN
MY YELLOW-AND-BLACK
ALIEN ALLIES!

TOP SECRET

NOWHERE,

EVERYWHERE,

PLANET HIDE-AND-SEEK

MORE THINGS TO DO

✳ Copy the five faces
you've matched into
the blank stamps.

✳ Can you spot three
yellow-and-black alien
friends of Odlaw's?
Keep your eyes peeled
for five more hiding in
the rest of this book!

WANDERING LINES

Look at all those blue Martians! Mark all the places where you can find three matching boxes in a row. They can be straight or diagonal. Odlaw found one already!

Gravity has made mayhem of these words!
Read the clues to help you unscramble the letters.

3. It's really big
SPACE

1. Another word for alien
EXTRATERRESTRIAL

2. Its size is unknown
UNIVERSE

4. Orbits Earth
MOON

7. Called the "Red Planet"
MARS

8. Lights up Earth
SUN

5. Something that orbits another object
SATELLITE

6. Drives a spacecraft
ASTRONAUT

12. Our galaxy (two words)
MILKY WAY

11. Has a tail
COMET

9. Star shine
TWINKLE

10. Instrument with glass lenses
TELESCOPE

MORE THINGS TO DO

* Spot a blue Martian who is asleep on a rock!

SPACE STATION DUPLICATION

Can you spot ten differences between each pair of scenes?

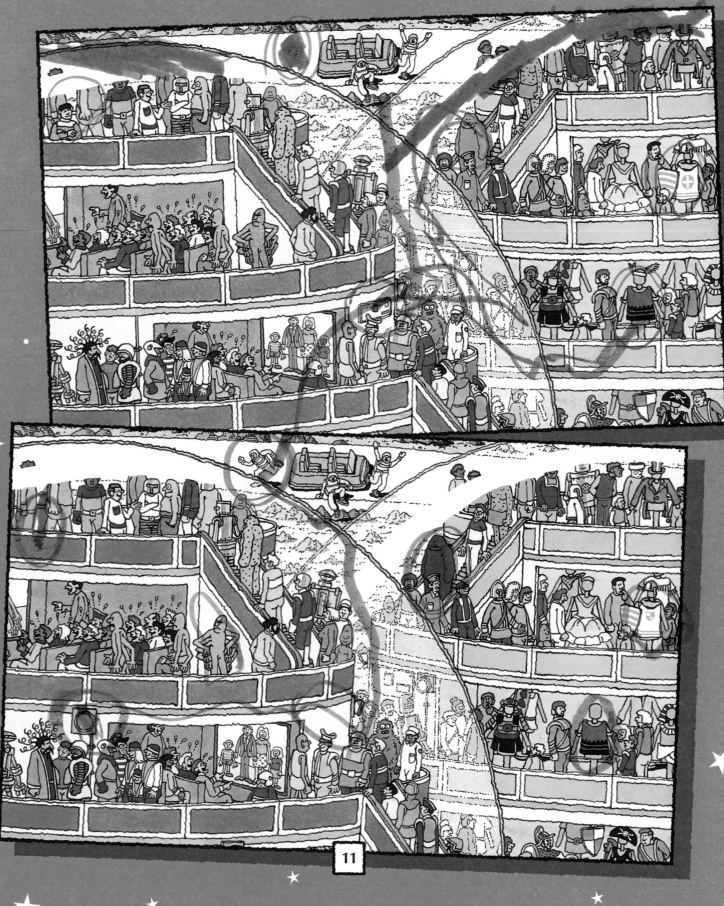

TELEPORTATION TANGLE

Beam me up! What a tangle! Follow the teleportation rays to find out who's traveling to which spaceship.

MORE THINGS TO DO

✳ How many books is Waldo holding? What space subjects might they be?

STRANGE CREATURE

Put Hungry Growler's face back together again by numbering the strips from 1 to 6.

HALF ALIEN, HALF . . .

What a bunch of crazy-looking creatures!
Can you pair up their top and bottom halves?

MORE THINGS TO DO

✴ Use a pencil and paper to trace this page, then cut up the characters' top and bottom halves to make new mixed-up creatures!

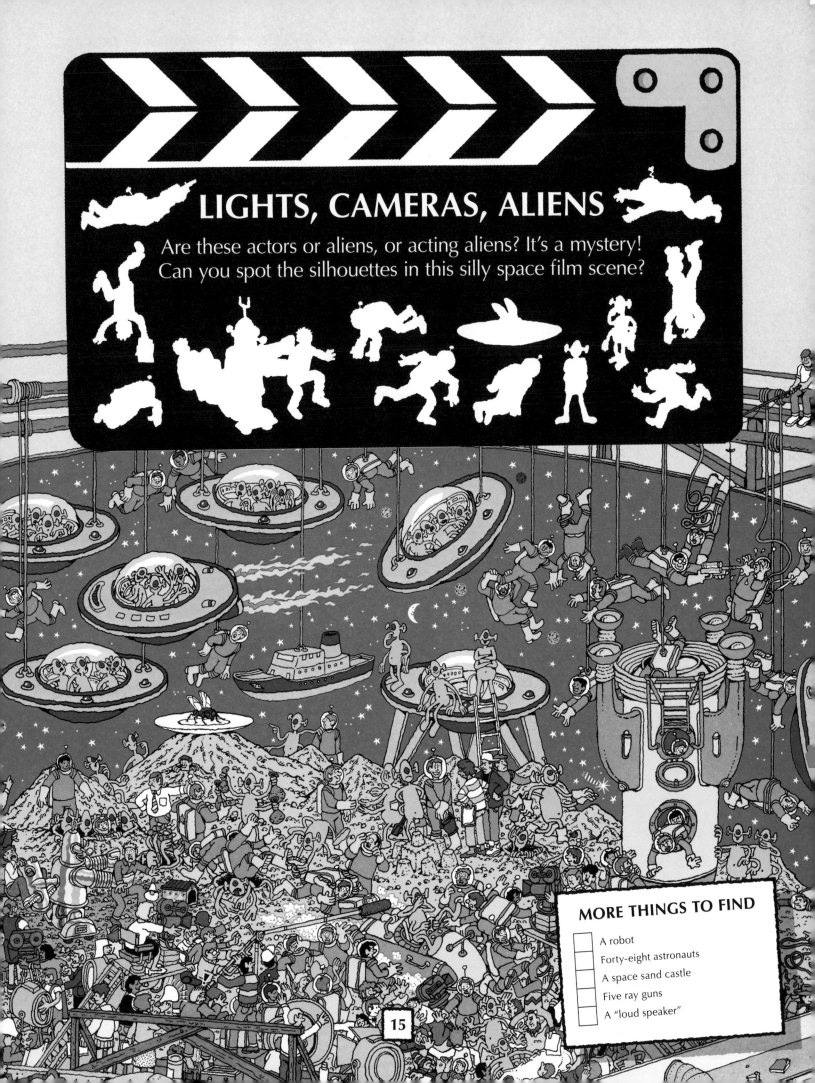

LIGHTS, CAMERAS, ALIENS

Are these actors or aliens, or acting aliens? It's a mystery!
Can you spot the silhouettes in this silly space film scene?

MORE THINGS TO FIND

- A robot
- Forty-eight astronauts
- A space sand castle
- Five ray guns
- A "loud speaker"

TIME AND SPACE MAZE

Help the yellow rocket find a route to the top, picking up all four crew members on the way. You can't pass clocks that have struck midnight! Tick, tock!

MORE THINGS TO FIND

☐ Three clocks with their numbers in the wrong order

☐ A clock that says five o'clock

☐ A clock with a number missing

STAR GAZE DAZE

Pair up any stars with pictures that seem similar and then spot the three differences between each pair. It's extra eye-boggling!

MORE THINGS TO DO

✱ Wenda loves the music of the stars. Can you find nine stars shaped like musical notes?

MOON MAYHEM

Help stop the hullabaloo on the planet of red and blue! Find the words in the moon of letters. The words go up, down, forward, and backward.

WORMHOLE
SUNSPOT
JETPACK
DUST
FULL MOON
NOVA

ORBIT
SPACE SUIT
ROBOT
VOYAGER
CRATER
PULSAR

OUT OF THIS WORLD

Transform me and my friends into marvelous Martians using wild and wacky colors!

SATELLITE SETS

Wow, it's crowded up here at night! Can you match each object in the sky with one or more identical copies—and reveal the one thing that is flying solo?

MORE THINGS TO FIND

- [ ] Six yellow cars
- [ ] Two fish
- [ ] Six thermometers
- [ ] Eighteen striped planets
- [ ] Two astronauts with wrenches

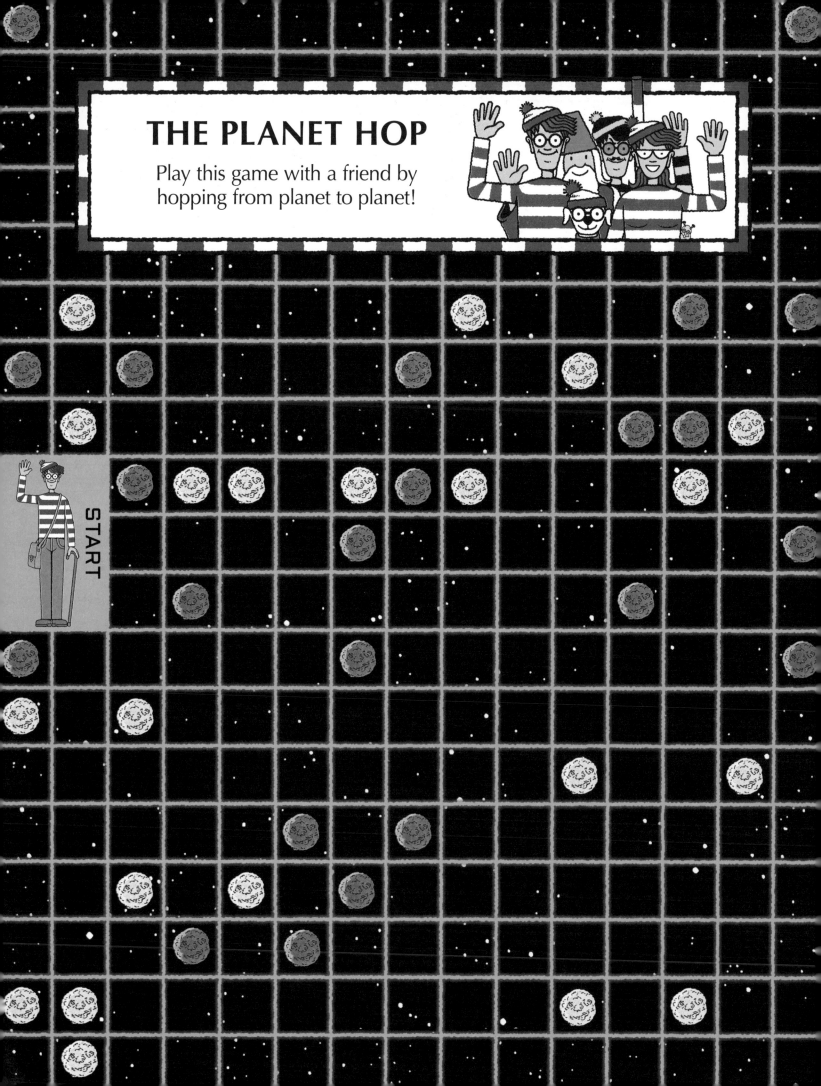

THE PLANET HOP

Play this game with a friend by
hopping from planet to planet!

START

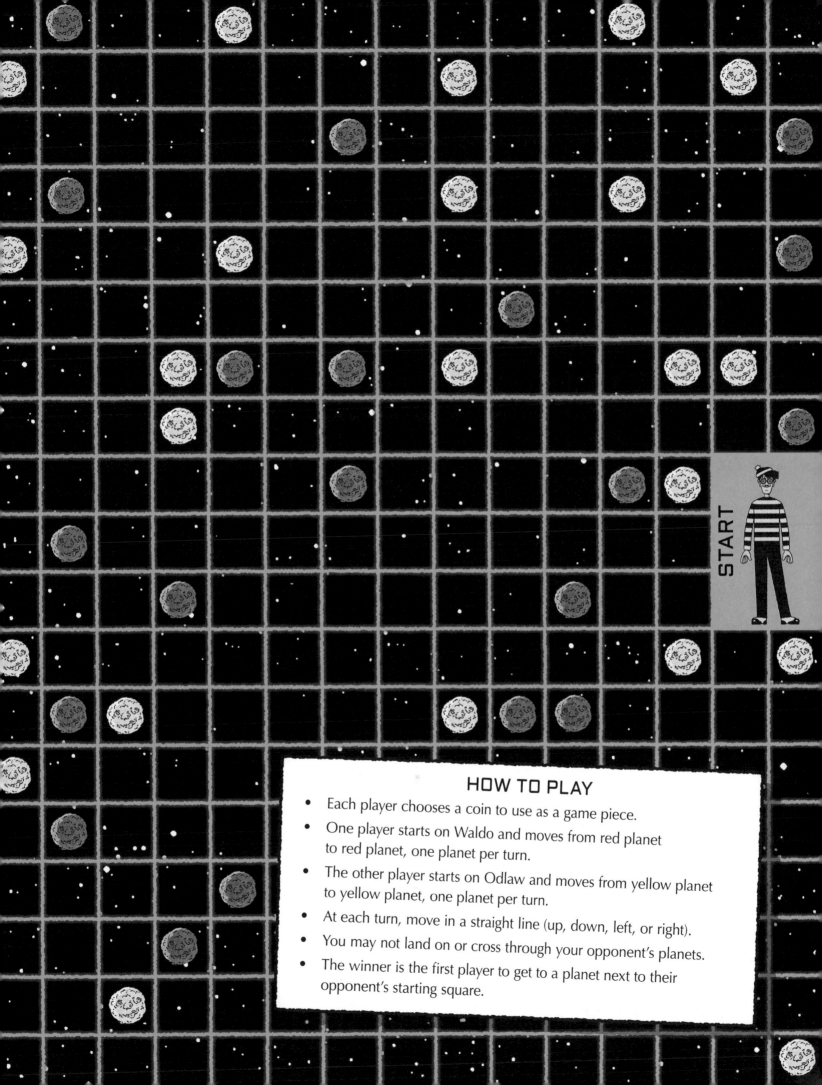

START

HOW TO PLAY

- Each player chooses a coin to use as a game piece.
- One player starts on Waldo and moves from red planet to red planet, one planet per turn.
- The other player starts on Odlaw and moves from yellow planet to yellow planet, one planet per turn.
- At each turn, move in a straight line (up, down, left, or right).
- You may not land on or cross through your opponent's planets.
- The winner is the first player to get to a planet next to their opponent's starting square.

MAKING CONTACT

Wow! The red planet is full of all sorts of secrets!
Use the decoder to read the magic messages.

WELL DONE, WALDO-WATCHERS! DID YOU FIND THE PRECIOUS STAR? IF NOT, THERE'S STILL TIME TO SEARCH FOR IT.

AND THERE'S MORE! SEE IF YOU CAN FIND THE ITEMS ON THE CHECKLIST IN THE STRIPED SHAPES BELOW.

WISHING YOU THE LUCK OF A THOUSAND STARS!

JOURNEY INTO OUTER SPACE CHECKLIST

- [ ] An alien with two heads
- [ ] A knife and fork
- [ ] An upside-down clock
- [ ] A green alien pointing
- [ ] Four pyramids
- [ ] A red book being read
- [ ] A pink alien with four legs
- [ ] A green man holding a silver shield
- [ ] Waldo writing with a pencil
- [ ] Thirteen green men on a bridge
- [ ] A Woof postage stamp
- [ ] An airplane not leaving a trail
- [ ] Fourteen man-shaped silhouettes
- [ ] Six bear constellations
- [ ] An astronaut wearing pink boots
- [ ] A green alien with a pink nose
- [ ] Four Waldo-watchers
- [ ] Thirty-two milk bottles
- [ ] A red-and-white umbrella
- [ ] A ship
- [ ] A three-eyed cat

ONE LAST THING . . .
Can you spot a meteor with a red-and-white striped tail and a meteor with a yellow-and-black striped tail? Happy hunti...

JOURNEY UP HIGH IN THE SKY!

NOW LET'S TAKE FLIGHT
ON AN AVIATION ADVENTURE PACKED
FULL OF LOOP-THE-LOOP CHAOS! POWER
UP THE ENGINES IN YOUR BRAIN SO THAT
YOU CAN PLAY THE PERPLEXING PUZZLES ALONG
THE WAY. SEARCH FOR A PHENOMENAL FEATHER
TOO. ENJOY THE BIRD'S-EYE VIEW, HIGHFLYERS!

FEATHER

DESTINATION EVERYWHERE

Unscramble the letters in the Destination column to spell the names of twelve cities. Then search for flights with "WAL" in them to find out which places I'll be traveling to. Wow!

Depart	Destination	Flight	Arrive	Delays
10:00	WEN OYKR	WAL1	22:00	ON TIME
08:00	NOONLD	WDA1	07:00	ON TIME
22:00	GNHO NKGO	WOF1	10:30	1 HOUR
11:30	RASIP	WOF2	21:00	ON TIME
23:00	BUDAI	ODW2	06:00	ON TIME
22:00	AOS AULOP	WAL2	10:00	ON TIME
13:00	STERAMDAM	WZD1	21:00	1 HOUR
21:00	OTONTOR	WZD2	23:00	ON TIME
23:00	KYOTO	WAL4	13:00	ON TIME
10:00	REOM	WAL3	23:00	ON TIME
19:00	SOLO	ODW1	22:00	3 HOURS
07:00	DNEYYS	WDA2	09:00	ON TIME

MORE THINGS TO DO

✸ Did Waldo catch all four flights? Starting with "WAL1," check the arrival time matches the departure time of "WAL2" and so on. Can you also find Wenda, Woof, Wizard Whitebeard, and Odlaw's abbreviated names, where they flew to, and if they caught their flights, too?

UP IN THE CLOUDS

Ta-da! Help Wizard Whitebeard hop to the finish by moving in repeated sequences of yellow, pink, white, and then blue clouds. He can only hop to a cloud that is next to the one he is on!

START

FINISH

HOT-AIR RACE

Clowns don't like to follow rules! Read the rules on the right to figure out which hot-air balloon is winning and which ones are disqualified. You'll go oogly-boogly-woogly-eyed!

To enter the race:

- A hot-air balloon must be manned by three clowns and no one else.
- One clown must wear a bow tie.
- A second clown must wear a top hat.
- A third clown must wear a red nose.
- Stripes or spots cannot be worn by the same clown.
- No pies allowed!
- A hot-air balloon basket must be the shape of a pom-pom hat.

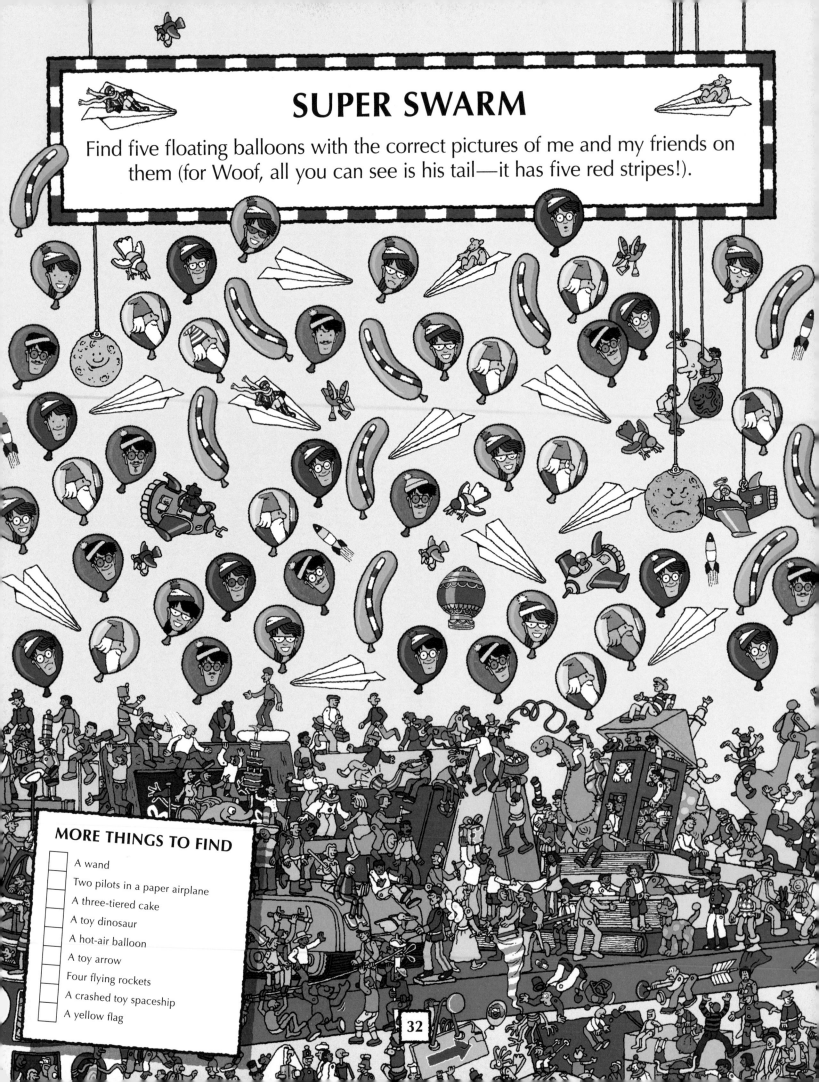

SUPER SWARM

Find five floating balloons with the correct pictures of me and my friends on them (for Woof, all you can see is his tail—it has five red stripes!).

MORE THINGS TO FIND

- [ ] A wand
- [ ] Two pilots in a paper airplane
- [ ] A three-tiered cake
- [ ] A toy dinosaur
- [ ] A hot-air balloon
- [ ] A toy arrow
- [ ] Four flying rockets
- [ ] A crashed toy spaceship
- [ ] A yellow flag

BIRD SEARCH
WORD SEARCH

Find the name of each feathered flying friend in this frame of letters. The words go forward, backward, and diagonally. Squawk!

O	O	K	C	U	C	W	D	P
U	R	C	V	B	O	K	R	V
M	E	D	L	R	O	M	I	U
E	K	A	C	T	I	W	B	L
W	C	R	G	L	A	A	G	T
	E	W	E	L	B	G	N	U
	P	I	D	G	E	T	I	R
	D	O	U	N	O	A	K	E
	O	V	E	O	M	I	C	C
	O	R	K	C	W	L	O	W
	A	W	D	L	L	U	G	M

Bird list:
- **Eagle**
- **Wren** • **Gull**
- **Crow** • **Cuckoo**
- **Mockingbird**
- **Woodpecker**
- **Vulture**
- **Emu**

MORE THINGS TO FIND

- ☐ The word *Odlaw*
- ☐ An upside-down pom-pom hat
- ☐ A dinosaur
- ☐ A very long snake
- ☐ Five monkeys
- ☐ Four bats
- ☐ Two witches
- ☐ Sixty-six yellow-and-black striped birds

BIRDS OF A FEATHER

Find one or more match for each flying creature, machine, person, or item in the sky to reveal the one left over.

MORE THINGS TO DO

* Tell this joke to a friend and see if it makes them laugh out loud:

Why does a seagull fly by the sea?

Because if it flew by the bay, it would be a bagel!

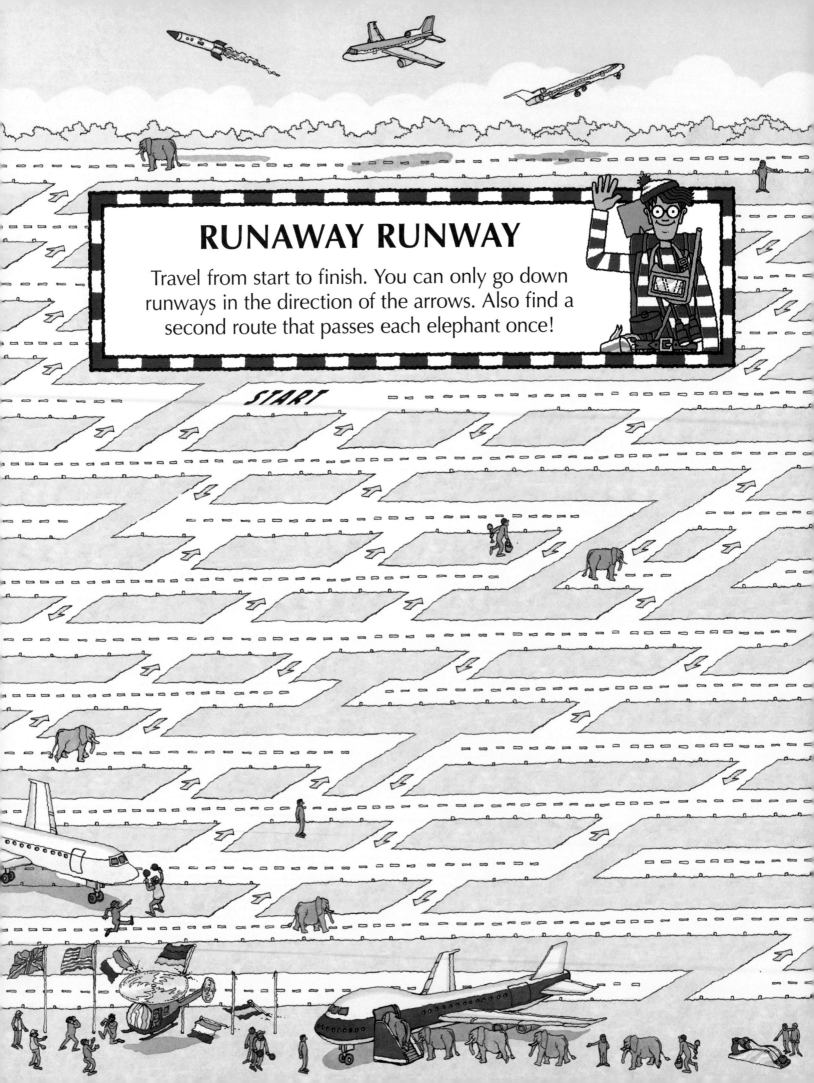

RUNAWAY RUNWAY

Travel from start to finish. You can only go down runways in the direction of the arrows. Also find a second route that passes each elephant once!

START

FINISH

MORE THINGS TO FIND

- A rocket
- A wind sock
- A flying ace
- An open suitcase
- A French flag
- Three buckets

DRAGON MEDAL MAYHEM

What a day of exciting races! Can you match each dragon to the medal they won? Read all seven descriptions closely and study the pictures on the medals for clues.

HANSEL DUSTY

This greedy dragon likes anything shiny and has a good sense of smell (but very bad breath!).

Sneakiness: high

Sense of direction: high

Strength: big claws for grabbing

THE FORTY WINKS RACE

SUNNY-SIDE-UP SID

This happy-go-lucky dragon likes to see things from a different perspective.

Sneakiness: low

Sense of direction: low

Intelligence: not so smart!

THE NUMBER CRUNCHING RACE
52
49

EDWINA SHARP

This dreadfully competitive dragon has a bad temper and an extra-pointy arrow tail.

Top speed: very fast

Battle power: high

Strength: long claws to sharpen swords

THE NAVIGATION RACE

CORNELIUS COMPASS

This witty dragon has sleek scales for aerodynamic tailwind.

Top speed: very fast

Sense of direction: exceptional; can read maps

Intelligence: high; likes to crack clever jokes!

THE UPSIDE-DOWN RACE

THE SWORD-FIGHTING RACE

COUNT BILL CRUNCH

This dragon is always hungry—for math!

Sneakiness: high

Strength: sharp fangs

Intelligence: high; can use his scales to count in multiples of nine

BUMP-IN-THE-NIGHT BERNIE

This scary dragon can float without flapping her wings. She likes to say "Boo!"

Sneakiness: exceptional; is a ghost

Strength: will grant wishes, if you can catch her

Intelligence: medium; can see through people

THE TREASURE HUNT RACE

THE NIGHT-FRIGHT RACE

SNOOZY VAN WINKLE

This toothless dragon prefers nighttime to day and can sleep for a year at a time.

Sense of direction: low

Tickle tolerance: low; giggles at the sight of feathers

Strength: raised yellow scales to soften the blow of bumping into things

COLOR SPLASH

It's nonstop flapping at the lighthouse for these flying dragons.
Not even goo guns can stop them! Color in this scene, if you dare!

BALLOON BINGO

Circle a number in the grid if you also see it on one of the ship balloons. Can you get five in a row?

1	7	18	6	12
25	19	2	15	21
10	3	17	22	5
14	8	11	23	16
9	20	24	13	4

MORE THINGS TO DO

* How did you win? Was it a line of vertical, horizontal, or diagonal numbers? Keep searching if you didn't get all three lines!

TAKEOFF TEN

What wacky airborne entertainment! Can you spot ten differences between each pair of scenes?

LUGGAGE LOOP

There's lots of chaos going on around this airport conveyor belt! Can you find your way through the luggage tags, lost luggage, and crowds of people to the finish?

Read the instructions before you set off.

- **Begin at the start and go forward either one or three squares.**

- **Move the number of squares as shown— but remember, a red luggage tag takes you backward and a yellow one forward. When you see both, you choose the direction.**

- **If you land on a square with a single suitcase, move to a matching square and then move forward five squares.**

- **If you land on a picture square, search for the image in the scene and then move forward five.**

FINISH

PLANE SNAP

Can you match up the plane playing cards to make eight pairs? Study each one very closely. Chocks away!

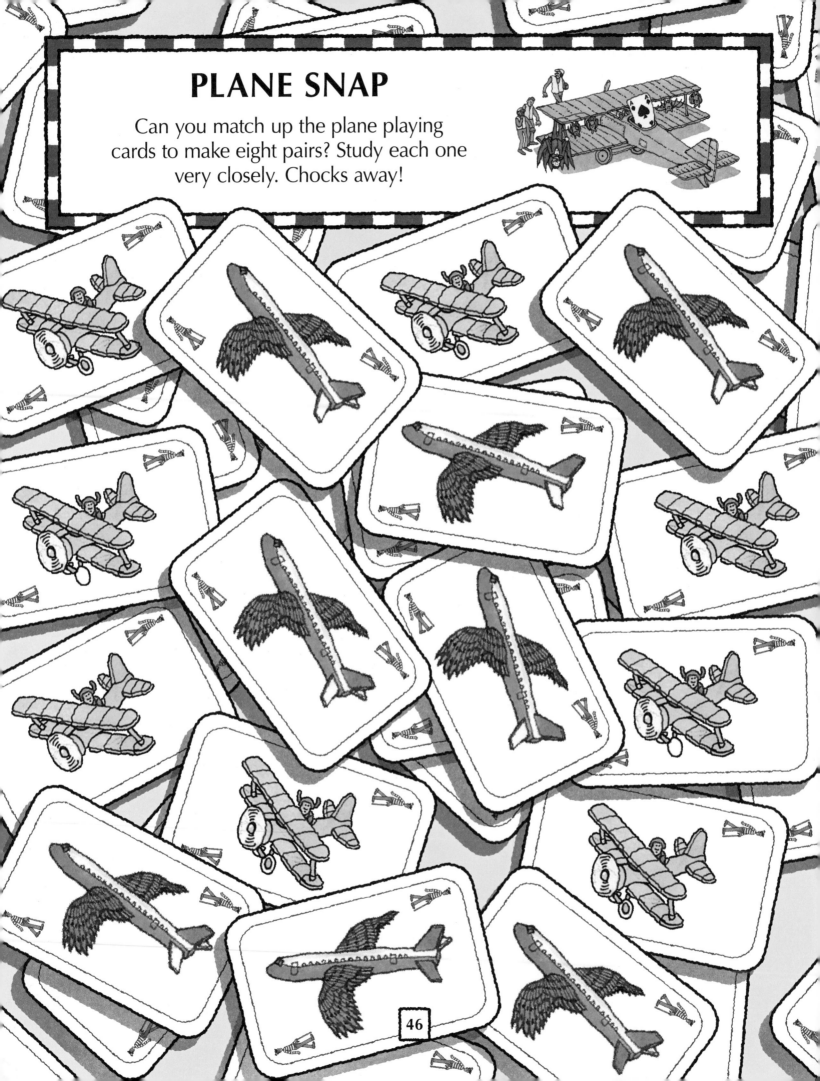

WELL DONE, WALDO-WATCHERS! DID YOU CATCH SIGHT OF THE FEATHER? IF NOT, THERE'S STILL TIME TO SEARCH FOR IT AGAIN!

WAIT, THERE'S MORE! LOOK BACK THROUGH THE PICTURES TO FIND THE ITEMS ON THE CHECKLIST AND SHOWN IN THE STRIPED SHAPES BELOW.

FULL SPEED AHEAD!

JOURNEY UP HIGH IN THE SKY CHECKLIST

- Three punctured hot-air balloons
- A red planet
- A suitcase of watches
- A suitcase with a broken handle
- A suitcase that's fallen on a man's foot
- A suitcase with two yellow stickers on it
- Six flight attendants wearing green uniforms
- Three pilots playing with toy airplanes
- A hanging sign with a red arrow
- Twenty-three flying silver spaceships
- Two telescopes pointed at each other
- A hand coming out of a chimney
- A dragon reading a *Where's Waldo?* book
- A bent telescope
- Thirteen paper airplanes
- Nine pink helicopters
- Two palm trees
- A red-spotted bandana
- A skiing clown
- A bent sword
- A mirror

ONE LAST THING . . .
Did you spot a balloon with a clown face on it? If not, then keep on looking until you do! The clown has a bright red nose! Honk, honk!

Journey across ancient lands!

IT'S TIME TO HOTFOOT IT ON A HIKE TO FARAWAY LANDS! WE'LL AMBLE ACROSS ANCIENT CITIES; ROAM THROUGH DEEP, DARK CAVES; AND SCALE CASTLE WALLS AS YOU SOLVE GREAT GAMES! WE'LL ALSO MEET CLEVER CLANS OF PEOPLE AND SOME MISCHIEVOUS MONSTERS! AND DON'T FORGET TO SEARCH NORTH, SOUTH, EAST, AND WEST FOR A PRECIOUS GEM. COMPASSES AND MAPS OUT, DEAR FRIENDS!

GEM

GREAT GUIDEBOOKS

Off we go! Cross out ten books that the riddles
rule out to reveal the one I'm taking on my travels.

STONE AGE ART

Animal Antics

The book you're looking for:

* Has no shields or swords . . .
* or anything made of bricks or stone.
* It's not about four-legged creatures.
* No cameras are allowed.
* Its travel tips go beyond the globe.
* It's full of mysteries, but they are not golden.
* Its route may (or may not!) take you north, south, east, or west.

HOW TO TAME A MONSTER

The Secrets of Ancient Gold

THE LAST DAYS OF THE AZTECS

TRAVELING THE WORLD

ANCIENT ROME

THE RIDDLE OF THE PYRAMIDS

MORE THINGS TO DO

* Keep your eyes peeled for lands on Waldo's route where some of these great guidebooks might be useful.

WENDA'S PHOTOGRAPHY GUIDE

At the Castle

ODLAW'S SNEAKY DIRECTIONS

GOING UNDERGROUND

Match the silhouettes to the people and creatures in these terrifying tunnels. Can you also find ten hidden gold coins? Make sure the monsters don't gobble you up!

THE TERRIFIC TEMPLE TREK

Follow my journey through Mexico until you find the
secret hiding place of the Aztec gold hoard.

❶ **Start your journey** by finding a Spanish conquistador holding
a flag with a double-headed eagle on it. ❷ **Walk along** the base of the
pyramid and climb up the tower of soldiers until you reach the man with
the very tall red-and-orange feather headdress. Be careful not to get hit
on the head! ❸ **Climb over** to the stairs at his right and run up to the
platform at the top. Greet the man wearing the four large feathers.

❹ **Slide down** the right-hand side of the stairs. Once you get past the falling rock, see if you can find the man with closed eyes holding a crossbow in one hand. ❺ **At ground level** walk to the right and find an Aztec warrior holding a yellow-and-black striped shield. Do you think he knows Odlaw?
❻ **Crawl over** to another dropped yellow-and-black striped shield. Avoid the falling man! ❼ **Jump onto** the gray horse and let the helmeted rider trot you around the corner. ❽ **Tiptoe up** the stairs to the top.
❾ **Dash into** the open mouth without being seen!

MORE THINGS TO FIND

- [ ] Nine birds
- [ ] Twenty-eight shields with feathers
- [ ] A man with his fingers in his ears
- [ ] Three men wearing gold medallions
- [ ] A pickpocket
- [ ] Eight men in yellow costumes with black spots

SURVIVAL SEQUENCES

Study the order of the pictures in the example, then fill in the blanks in games 1, 2, and 3. (The sequence starts over again when it reaches the end symbol.)

MORE THINGS TO DO

❋ Draw your own stick-figure sequence!

CAVE LIFE QUIZ

We stumbled upon amazing caves! Here are questions to bamboozle your brain. Some have more than one answer!

1. The Stone Age is called the Stone Age because:
- ☐ tools were made of stone
- ☐ beds were made of rocks
- ☐ dinosaurs threw stones

2. During this time, the people:
- ☐ hunted and gathered food
- ☐ didn't hunt for food
- ☐ got takeout

3. Found on cave walls were:
- ☐ paintings of animals
- ☐ magic doors
- ☐ paintings of dragons

4. Found in caves were:
- ☐ bears
- ☐ baboons
- ☐ lions

5. Mastodons looked like:
- ☐ elephants
- ☐ mice
- ☐ dogs

6. These things were woolly:
- ☐ rhinos
- ☐ mammoths
- ☐ fish

7. Cave dwellers knew how to make:
- ☐ fire
- ☐ origami
- ☐ lasagna

8. Wild boars are most closely related to:
- ☐ platypuses
- ☐ porcupines
- ☐ pigs

9. Animal skin and bones were used to make:
- ☐ clothes
- ☐ tools
- ☐ dish detergent

10. Handmade tools included:
- ☐ shields
- ☐ spears
- ☐ swords

MORE THINGS TO FIND
- ☐ Two red apples
- ☐ Ten cave dogs
- ☐ Two cave bears

FOOTSTEP FINDS

Start on a character square and follow their footstep guide to find out who wandered where.

MORE THINGS TO FIND

Who landed by a;

- [ ] cake;
- [ ] spooky doorway;
- [ ] man with ticklish feet;
- [ ] hole in the ground;
- [ ] stone statue?

BUILDING BLOCKS

It's crazy and cryptic construction time! Can you complete each grid using only the shaped blocks shown underneath it?

HINT: If you get stuck, copy the pieces onto grid paper and cut them out to try different combinations until you get it right!

MORE THINGS TO DO

✳ Color in the blocks once you've figured out the answers!

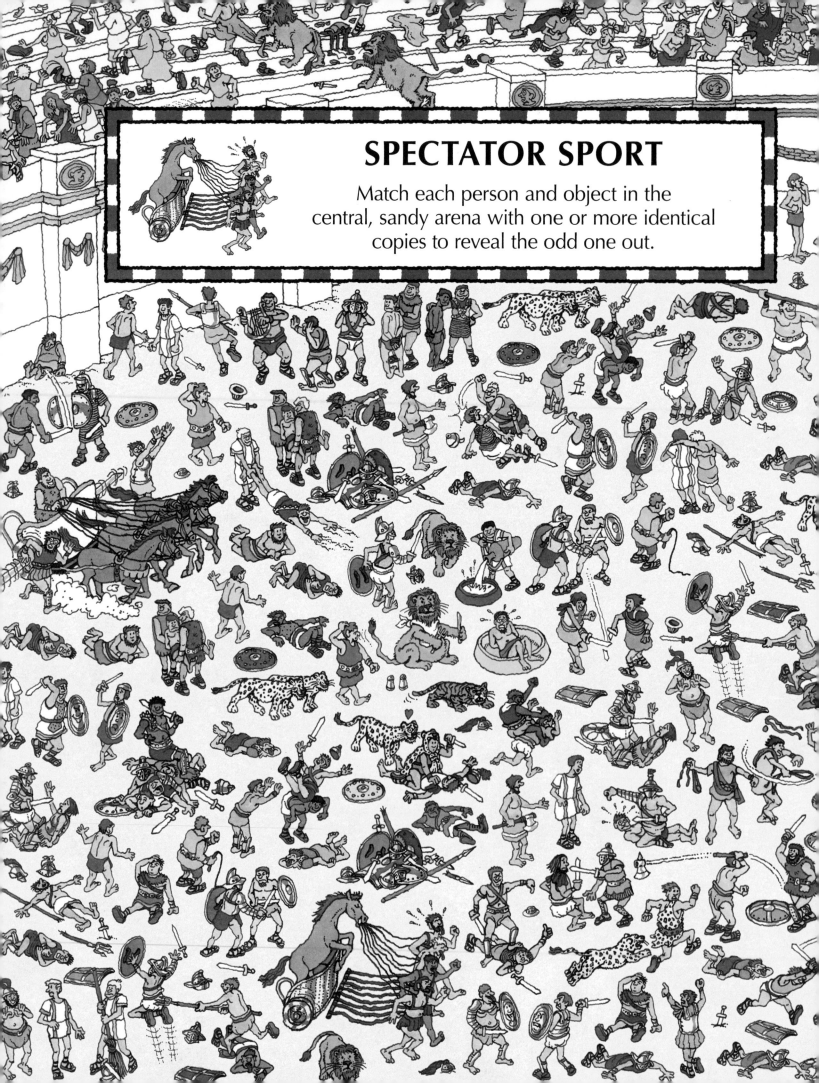

SPECTATOR SPORT

Match each person and object in the central, sandy arena with one or more identical copies to reveal the odd one out.

MORE THINGS TO DO

✴ Draw sandals on some of the Romans' bare feet!

✴ Think up tricks for taming lions, leopards, and tigers.

SCALING LADDERS

Fill in the missing words! Start at the top and change only one letter at a time (the rest of the letters stay in the same order).

WALL

_ _ _ _

_ _ _ _

FEEL

BOTTLE

_ _ _ _ _ _

_ _ _ _ _ _

T L E
_ _ _ _ _ _

↑

See pages 56 and 66 for a clue to the word above!

MORE THINGS TO FIND

☐ A ladder with eleven rungs
☐ Two striped shields
☐ Three cats

MONSTER MAYHEM

Yikes! Helmeted hunters are lost in a monstrous land!
What do you think they are saying, dreaming, singing, or yelling?

RIGHT-ANGLED ANIMALS

What creatures lurk in this fantastic forest? Trace and cut out the shaped pieces below and use them to make the animals on the opposite page.

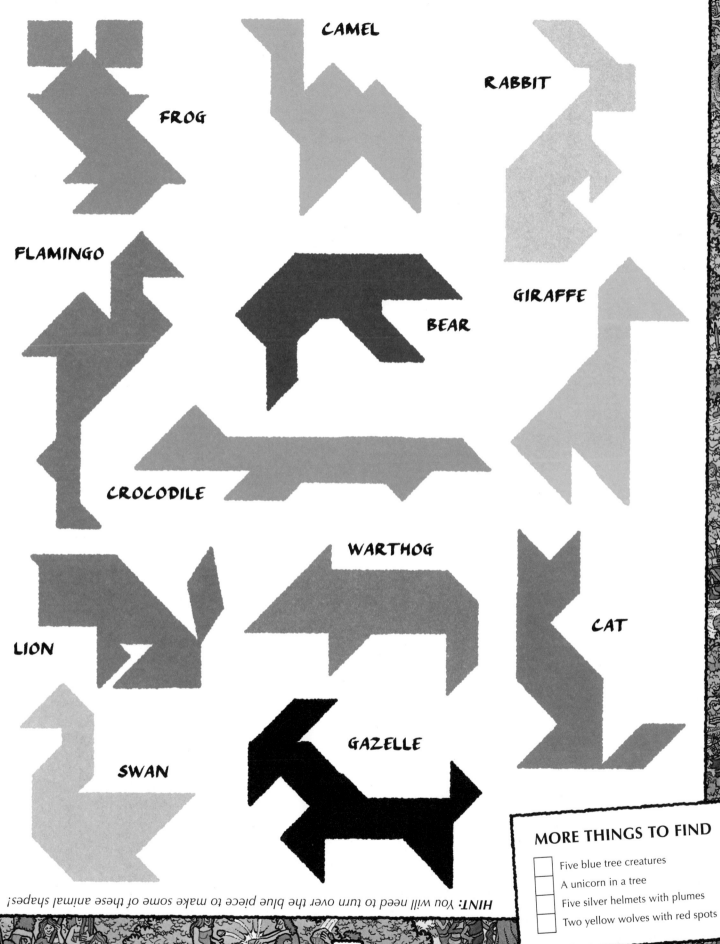

CAMEL

RABBIT

FROG

FLAMINGO

GIRAFFE

BEAR

CROCODILE

WARTHOG

CAT

LION

GAZELLE

SWAN

HINT: *You will need to turn over the blue piece to make some of these animal shapes!*

MORE THINGS TO FIND

- [ ] Five blue tree creatures
- [ ] A unicorn in a tree
- [ ] Five silver helmets with plumes
- [ ] Two yellow wolves with red spots

WRITE LIKE AN EGYPTIAN

Decode the ancient messages using the scroll of hieroglyphics.
Then write your name in the blank scroll.

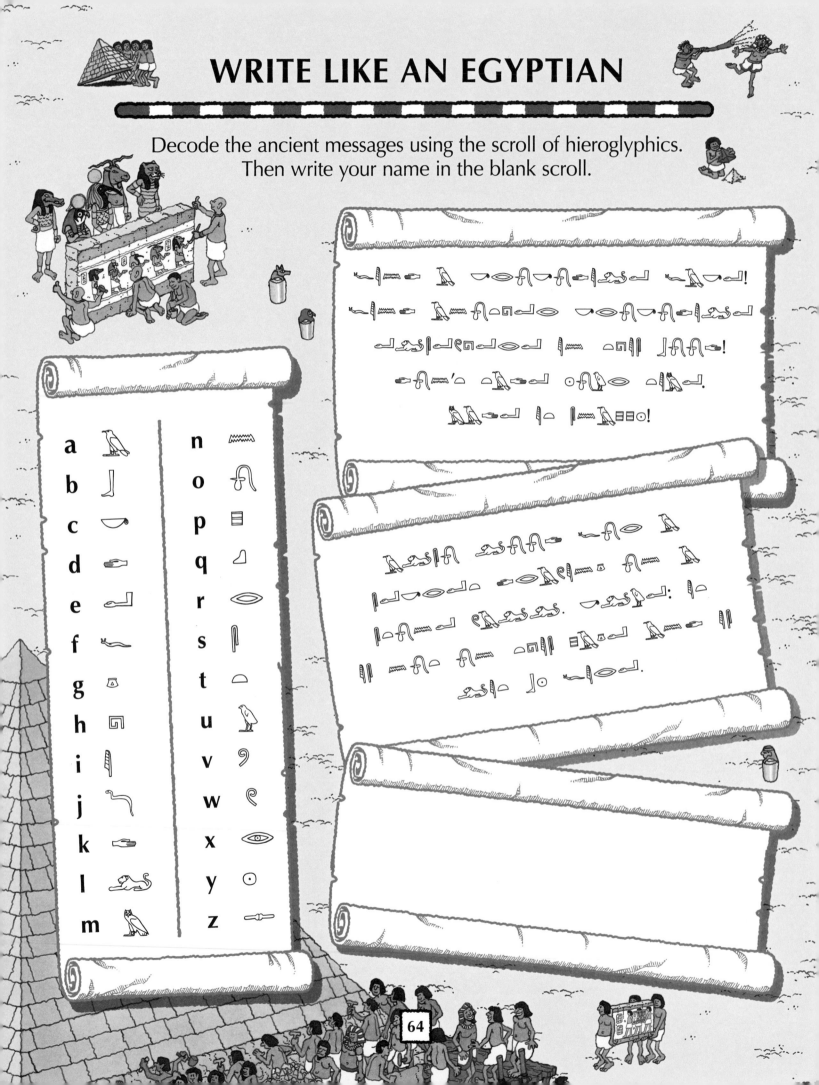

IMAGINE YOUR CITY!

Use the triangles as a guide to build and color
in your very own Egyptian city.

COUNT OF THE CASTLE

Find a way to the finish to free the
prisoners locked in the castle towers!
You can play by yourself or with friends.

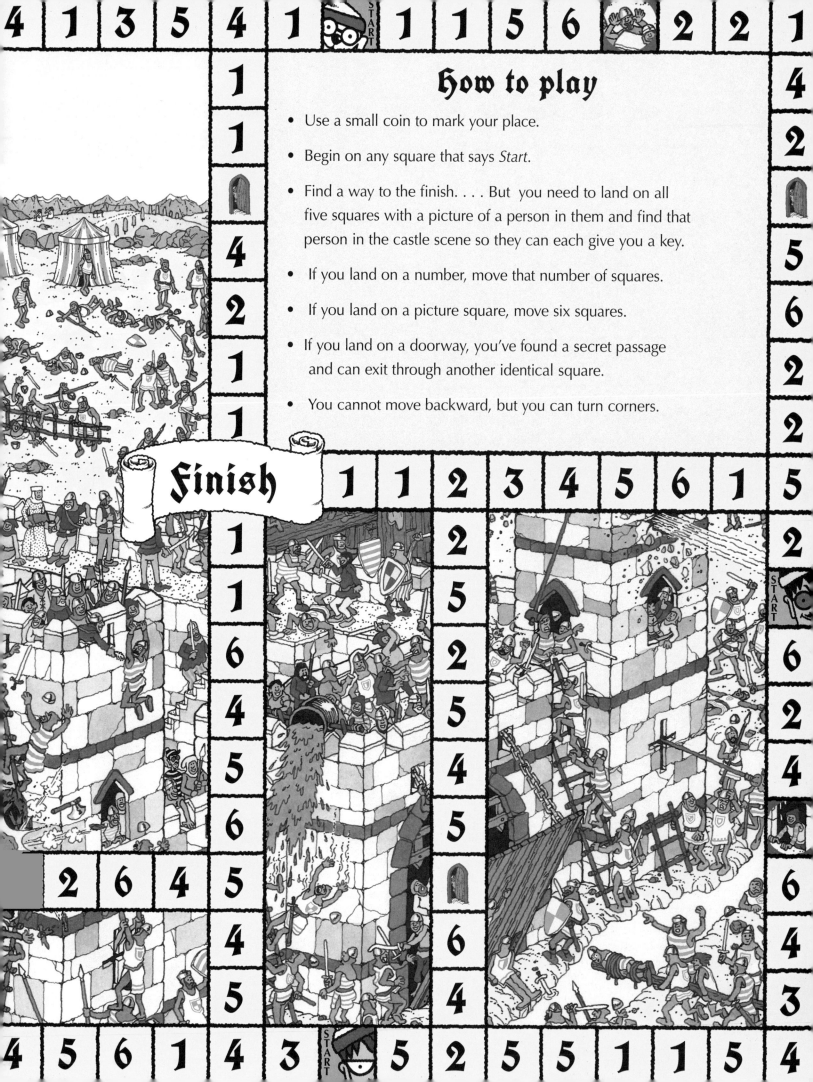

How to play

- Use a small coin to mark your place.

- Begin on any square that says *Start*.

- Find a way to the finish. . . . But you need to land on all five squares with a picture of a person in them and find that person in the castle scene so they can each give you a key.

- If you land on a number, move that number of squares.

- If you land on a picture square, move six squares.

- If you land on a doorway, you've found a secret passage and can exit through another identical square.

- You cannot move backward, but you can turn corners.

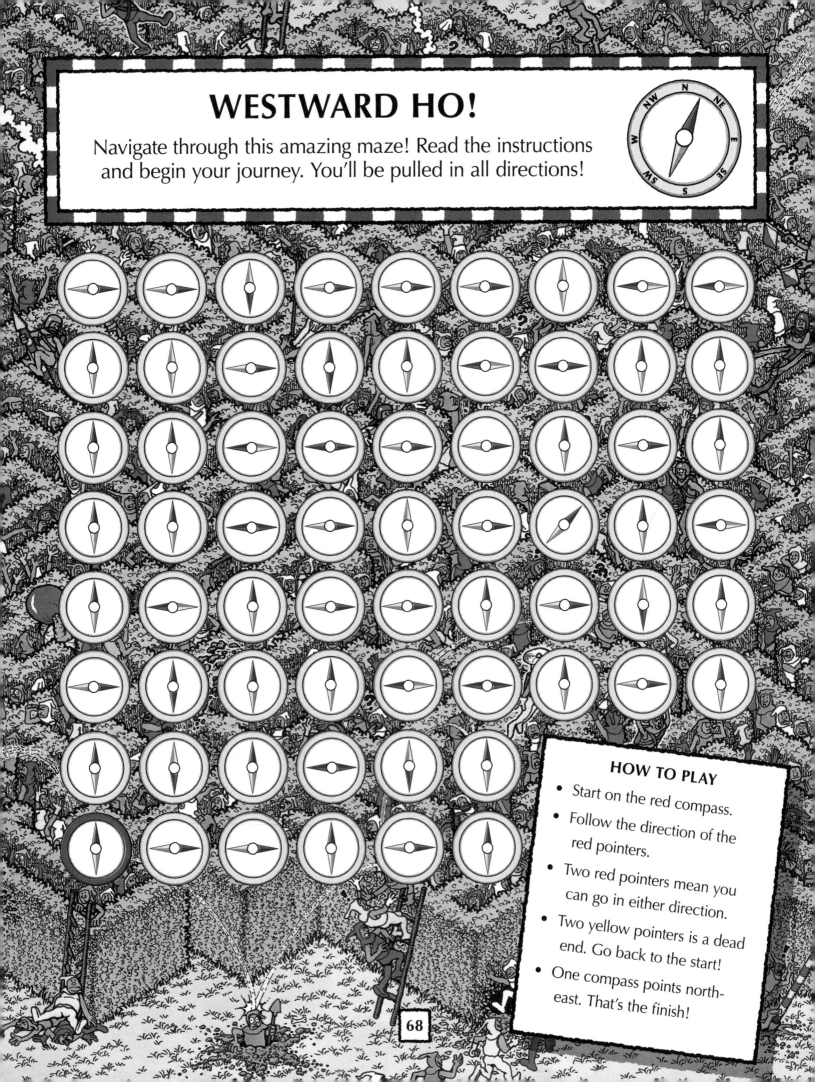

WELL DONE, WALDO-WATCHERS! DID YOU FIND THE GREAT GEM TREASURE? IF NOT, THERE'S STILL TIME TO SEARCH FOR IT!

WAIT, THERE'S MORE! LOOK BACK THROUGH THE PICTURES TO FIND THE ITEMS ON THE CHECKLIST AND SHOWN IN THE STRIPED SHAPES BELOW. IT'S TIME TO HOP, SKIP, AND JUMP YOUR WAY BACK TO THE BEGINNING!

JOURNEY ACROSS ANCIENT LANDS CHECKLIST

- A sitar player
- Five trees with faces
- A message in a bottle
- Five fair maidens in a line
- A landscape painting
- Four broken ladders
- A green dragon
- Three muddy mudslingers
- Two witches
- A pyramid sandcastle
- A mermaid
- A wooden mallet
- A man with his feet in stocks
- Two tipped cauldrons
- A flag with eight faces
- Two bent swords
- Three flattened knights
- A globe
- Cave clothes hung out to dry
- A fire-breathing gargoyle
- A skipping monster

ONE LAST THING . . .
Did you find a shield with Waldo's red-and-white pom-pom hat? And did you find another with Odlaw's yellow-and-black pom-pom hat? Keep searching!

Journey out to sea!

COME WITH ME ON A WET AND WILD ADVENTURE! WE'LL "SEA" (HA, HA!) SO MANY PEOPLE ON THE BEACH AND IN THE WATER, INCLUDING PESKY PIRATES AND VILLAINOUS

TO:
WALDO-MATES,
DOWN THE PLUGHOLE,
UP THE CREEK

VIKINGS ON THE HUNT FOR TREASURE. WATCH OUT FOR CRAZY UNDERWATER CREATURES TOO! INCREDIBLE! THERE ARE LOTS OF FIN-TASTIC GAMES FOR YOU TO PLAY,

AND THEY'RE ALL COMPLETELY BARNACLES! CAN YOU HELP ME FIND THE LAST TREASURE, A PRECIOUS SHELL? ANCHORS AWEIGH!

SHELL

SEA SILHOUETTES

Study this busy beach scene to find each silhouette. Wow, what a sizzling search!

GONE FISHING

Who caught a jellyfish? Also, find one fish within each school of yellow, pink, blue, and green fish with different-colored fins.

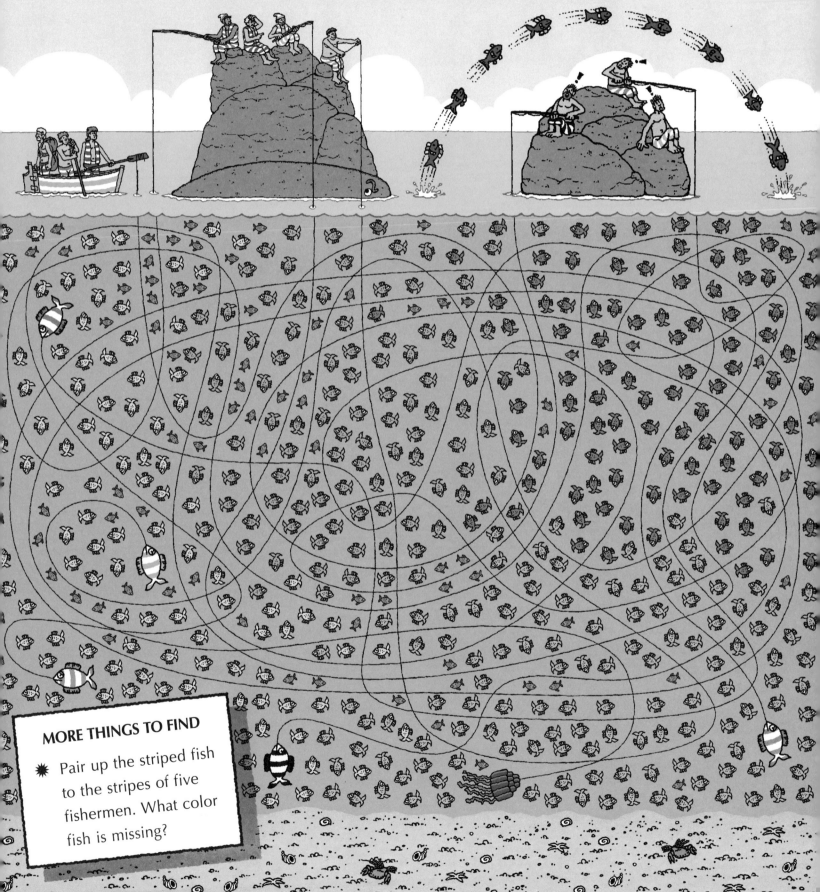

MORE THINGS TO FIND

✳ Pair up the striped fish to the stripes of five fishermen. What color fish is missing?

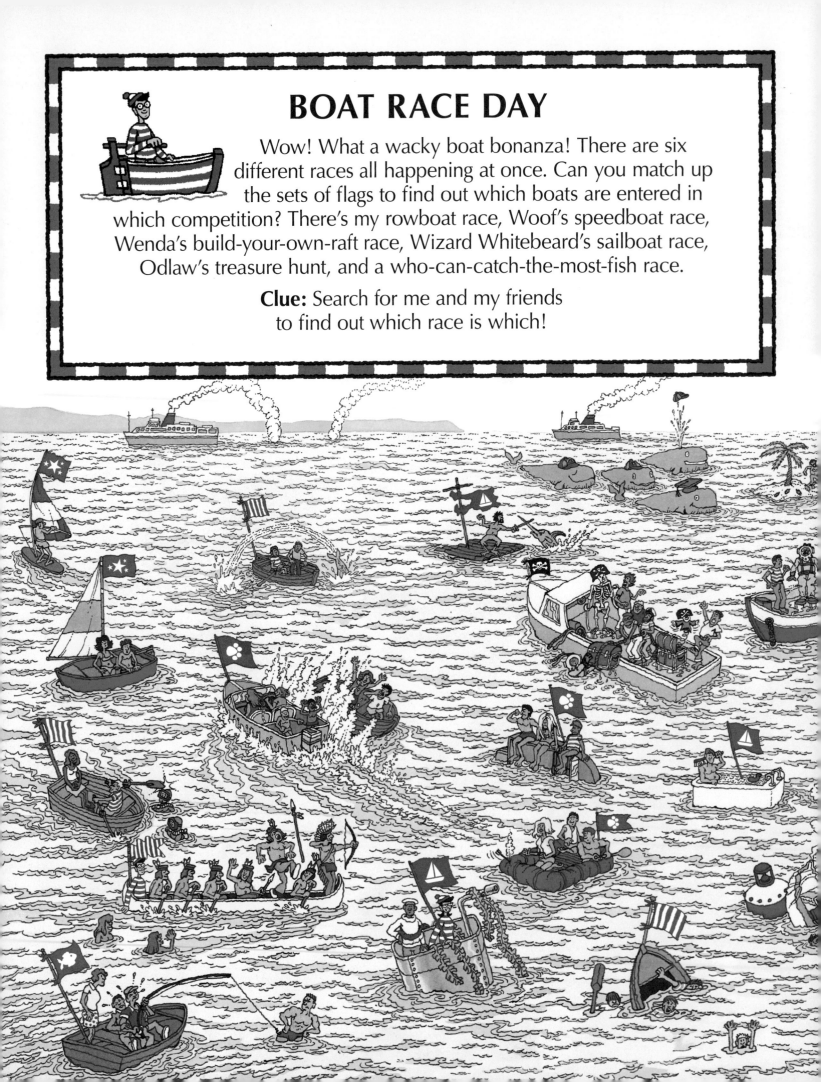

BOAT RACE DAY

Wow! What a wacky boat bonanza! There are six different races all happening at once. Can you match up the sets of flags to find out which boats are entered in which competition? There's my rowboat race, Woof's speedboat race, Wenda's build-your-own-raft race, Wizard Whitebeard's sailboat race, Odlaw's treasure hunt, and a who-can-catch-the-most-fish race.

Clue: Search for me and my friends to find out which race is which!

SECRET SWIMATHON

Follow my wanders across the open waters until you
find the one boat with treasure stashed onboard.

❶ **First,** find a boat with a trail of steam that rises in and out of the water.
❷ **Jump overboard** and swim to a "school." Have a whale of a time!
❸ **Continue** on past a swordfight, to a man wearing a three-feathered
headdress. ❹ **"Duck" underwater** to something that is rubber and red
but not inflatable. ❺ **Swim behind** a "sea bed" to mermaids. Avoid
the tangled water-skiers! ❻ **Find** a bull and he will help you aboard!

THE TREASURE TRAMPLE

First, find me. From there, draw a straight line passing through all five of my coordinates. Then do the same for Odlaw and Wenda. Can you find the square where we all cross paths? Pirate treasure is buried there!

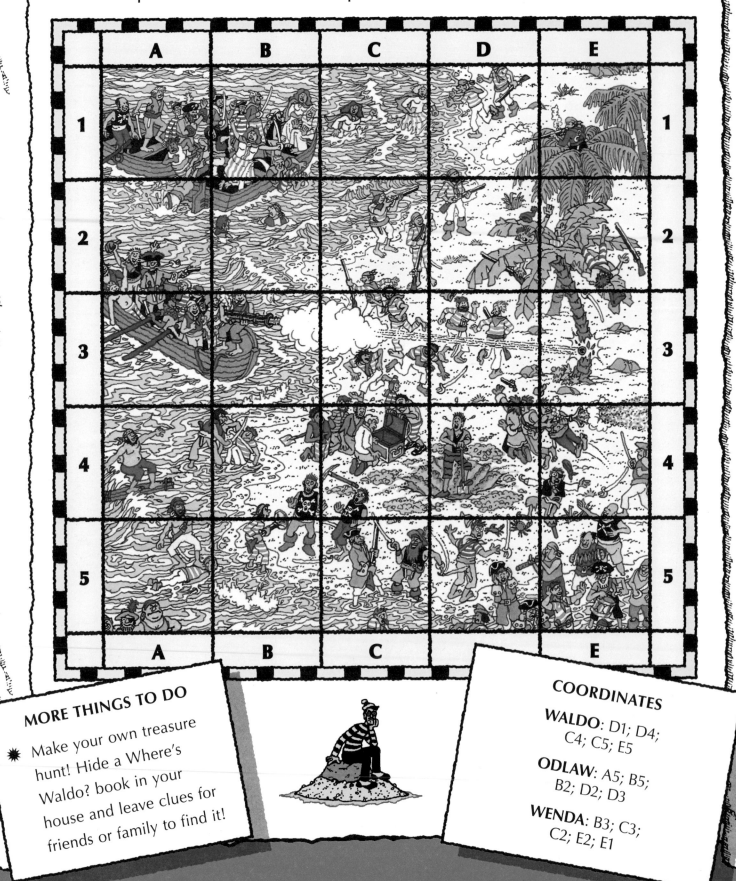

MORE THINGS TO DO

✹ Make your own treasure hunt! Hide a Where's Waldo? book in your house and leave clues for friends or family to find it!

COORDINATES

WALDO: D1; D4; C4; C5; E5

ODLAW: A5; B5; B2; D2; D3

WENDA: B3; C3; C2; E2; E1

NORSE CODE

Decode the second message to help you find a treasure map on this page. Start by copying over any letters with the same Norse letter, then fill in the blanks.

MESSAGE ONE

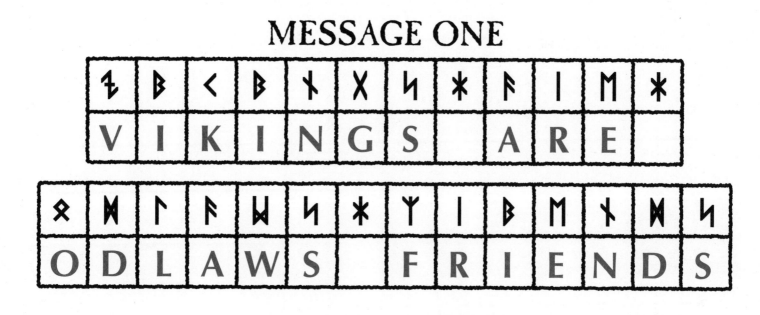

V	I	K	I	N	G	S		A	R	E

O	D	L	A	W	S		F	R	I	E	N	D	S

MESSAGE TWO

SNAKY SEARCH

Find the *S* words in the word search below. Letters must run continuously, but they can go in any direction as long as the sides of their squares touch. Sssneaky!

Stripes
Slippery
Sea snake
Scaly skin
Spots
Snakebite

MORE THINGS TO FIND

* One repeated word that is backward.

* A word that isn't a snake (but you might mistake it for one!).

FISH FOOD

Look behind you! Who is going to eat who? Put these pictures in order by numbering them from 1 to 7.

MORE THINGS TO DO

✹ Draw your own comic strip on a piece of paper. Then cut out the frames, mix them up, and ask friends or family to place them in sequence!

✹ Can you spot one goldfish in the background with a different-shaped tail?

PIECES OF EIGHT

Look closely at the pictures in the coins to find out which ones are in the scene. Be warned, four of them are from elsewhere in the book! Yo, ho, ho!

MORE THINGS TO DO

＊ Being a pirate is all about luck! Toss a coin: heads, you're a pirate; tails, you're a fisherman!

SEASHELLS GALORE

I see seashells on the seashore! Seek out and color in only the shells ◯,
not the pebbles ◯, to reveal four items washed ashore.

MORE THINGS TO DO

✳ At the beach, collect
flat stones (the size of a
quarter). With a friend,
take turns stacking one
stone at a time. The
winner is the one who
doesn't topple the tower.

SEA SETS

Match each sea creature, scuba diver, and item under the sea with one or more identical copies to find an odd one out. It's maritime mayhem down there!

MORE THINGS TO DO

* Can you solve these riddles?

What do you call a fish without an eye? "fsh"

How do you make an octopus laugh? With ten-tickles

PIRATEY PUZZLE

Avast, me hearties! What a puzzling picture! Can you find the correct three missing pieces? Arrr!

MESSAGE IN A BOTTLE

Find eight real words or phrases by matching up the pairs of papers. Write your answers in the bottle. You can use each piece more than once. Four pairs of ripped edges fit together perfectly.

BLOCK

SAND

SHIP

HORSE

GLASSES

PIRATE

CASTLE

SHELL

SEA

QUICK

SUN

WRECK

1. ....
2. ....
3. ....
4. ....
5. ....
6. ....
7. ....
8. ....

MAKE A MONSTROSITY

Create your very own sea creature and color in the surrounding scene. What do you think is lurking at the bottom of this deep, dark sea? Eeek!

FISHING NET SETS

What a catch! Draw in the missing symbols. All nine must appear once in each box, but never in the same row.

DEEP-SEA DIVE

Choose a start picture. Then move to any square that shares one identical creature (including color). The squares do not have to be touching. Keep going until you find a combination that gets you to a finish. Your moves will take you all over the place! You can go diagonally, down and up and down again, and jump however many rows you like.

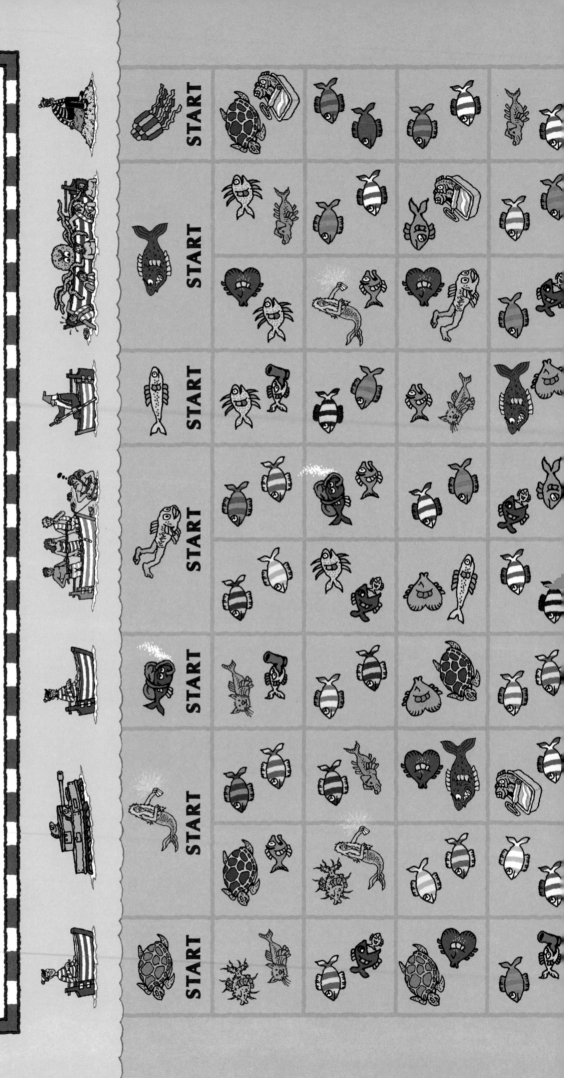

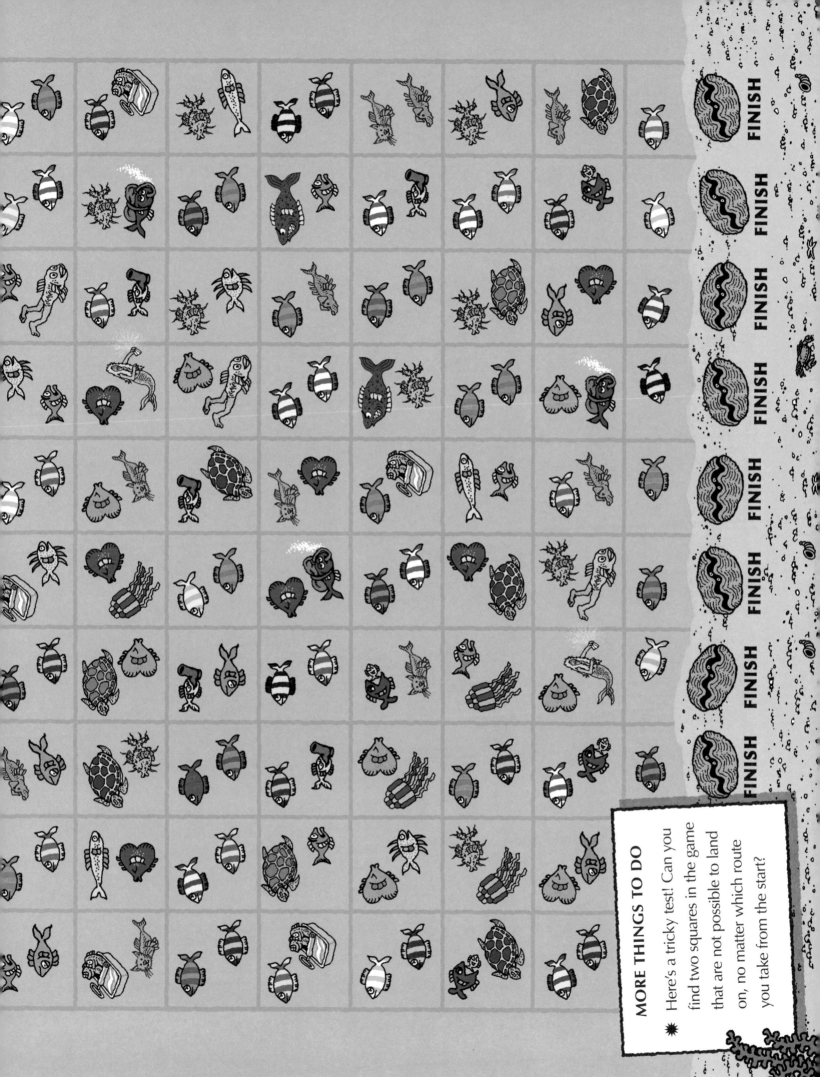

FINISH **FINISH** **FINISH** **FINISH** **FINISH** **FINISH** **FINISH** **FINISH**

MORE THINGS TO DO

✷ Here's a tricky test! Can you find two squares in the game that are not possible to land on, no matter which route you take from the start?

BLOWING BUBBLES

Glug, glug! Cross out the three letters that spell the word *pop* in each bubble. Then unscramble the rest of the letters to spell eleven words.

MORE THINGS TO FIND

- A yellow starfish
- A bucket
- Woof's tail
- Five swimmers wearing green stripes

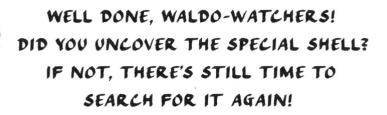

WELL DONE, WALDO-WATCHERS!
DID YOU UNCOVER THE SPECIAL SHELL?
IF NOT, THERE'S STILL TIME TO
SEARCH FOR IT AGAIN!

WAIT, THERE'S MORE! LOOK BACK
THROUGH THE PICTURES TO FIND
THE ITEMS ON THE CHECKLIST AND
SHOWN IN THE SHAPES BELOW.

HAVE EEL-Y GOOD FUN!

JOURNEY OUT TO SEA CHECKLIST

- [ ] Eighteen orange crabs
- [ ] A punctured raft
- [ ] Two men falling out of a palm tree
- [ ] A man-shaped hole in a pirate ship's sail
- [ ] Fish jumping through a boat's sail
- [ ] A cowboy riding a sea horse
- [ ] A fish with five boat-shaped silhouettes on its side
- [ ] A whale disguised as a rock
- [ ] An island surrounded by sharks
- [ ] Five sea "lions"
- [ ] Eight electric eels
- [ ] Three green octopuses
- [ ] Two men hooked by fishing lines
- [ ] A red-and-yellow umbrella
- [ ] Two fish "tanks"
- [ ] A fishbowl
- [ ] Six "saw" fish
- [ ] Three beach balls
- [ ] Three pirates with hooks for hands
- [ ] Two fish wearing pom-pom hats
- [ ] Waldo, Woof, Wenda, Wizard Whitebeard, and Odlaw hiding behind seaweed

ONE LAST THING . . .
Did you spot a fish that Wizard Whitebeard made with his magic? It's red, white, and blue and has stars on it too. Wow!

WOW! WONDERFUL! WELL DONE! WHAT A TERRIFIC TREASURE HUNT!
DID YOU FIND THE STAR, THE FEATHER, THE GEM, AND THE SHELL? DID
YOU ALSO REMEMBER TO LOOK FOR MY KEY, WOOF'S BONE, WENDA'S
CAMERA, WIZARD WHITEBEARD'S SCROLL, AND ODLAW'S BINOCULARS
IN EACH OF THE FOUR DESTINATIONS? IF YOU DIDN'T SPOT THEM
FIRST TIME AROUND, GO BACK AND SEE IF YOU CAN FIND THEM.

THERE ARE ANSWERS TO SOME OF THE HARDEST PUZZLES
ON THE OPPOSITE PAGE. DON'T GIVE UP ON THE OTHERS.
WHY NOT ASK YOUR FRIENDS TO HELP IF YOU GET STUCK?

Waldo

ANSWERS

JOURNEY INTO OUTER SPACE!

p. 8 WANDERING LINES

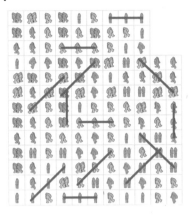

p. 9 WORD WORLDS

1. Extraterrestrial 2. Universe 3. Space 4. Moon
5. Satellite 6. Astronaut 7. Mars 8. Sun 9. Twinkle
10. Telescope 11. Comet 12. Milky Way

p. 12 TELEPORTATION TANGLE

p. 16 TIME AND SPACE MAZE

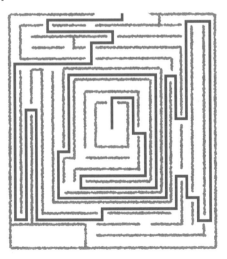

p. 18 MOON MAYHEM

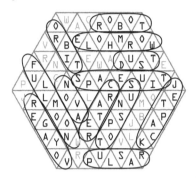

p. 24 MAKING CONTACT

Top: There are thirty-six red aliens in this book. Help me find them all! *Middle:* See if you can also spot a planet with seven red aliens standing on it. *Bottom:* Locate five red-hooded monks shooting fire. I'm in my favorite colored spaceship on that page.

JOURNEY UP HIGH IN THE SKY!

p. 28 DESTINATION EVERYWHERE

Waldo went from New York to São Paulo to Rome to Toyko. Wenda went from London to Sydney. Woof went from Hong Kong to Paris. Wizard Whitebeard left from Amsterdam but missed his flight in Toronto. Odlaw left from Oslo but missed his flight in Dubai.

p. 29 UP IN THE CLOUDS

pp. 30–31 HOT-AIR RACE

p. 33 BIRD SEARCH WORD SEARCH

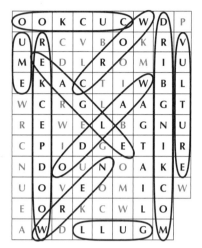

pp. 36–37 RUNAWAY RUNWAY

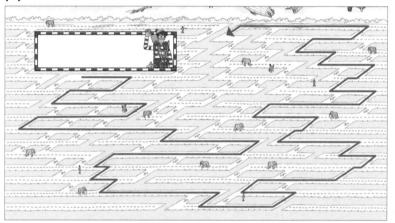

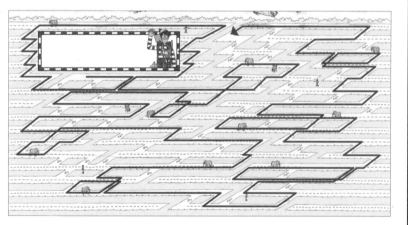

p. 41 BALLOON BINGO

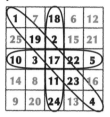

JOURNEY ACROSS ANCIENT LANDS!

p. 50 GREAT GUIDEBOOKS

p. 55 CAVE LIFE QUIZ

1. Tools were made of stone 2. Hunted and gathered food 3. Paintings of animals
4. Bears & Lions 5. Elephants
6. Rhinos & Mammoths 7. Fire 8. Pigs
9. Clothes & Tools 10. Spears

p. 57 BUILDING BLOCKS

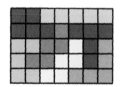

p. 60 SCALING LADDERS

WALL → **F**ALL → F**E**LL → FE**E**L
BOTTLE → B**A**TTLE → **C**ATTLE → CA**S**TLE

pp. 62–63 RIGHT-ANGLED ANIMALS

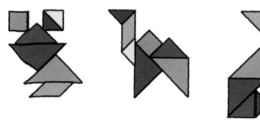

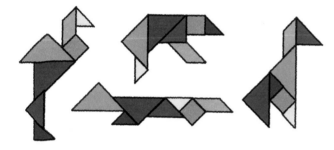

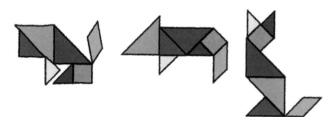

p. 64 WRITE LIKE AN EGYPTIAN

Top: Find a crocodile face! Find another crocodile elsewhere in this book! Don't take your time. Make it snappy! *Middle:* Also look for a secret drawing on a stone wall. *Clue:* It is not on this page and is lit by fire.

JOURNEY OUT TO SEA!

p. 73 GONE FISHING

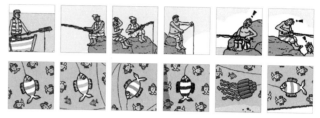

A red striped fish is missing.

p. 74 BOAT RACE DAY

Waldo's rowboat race

Woof's speedboat race

Wenda's build-your-own-raft race

Wizard Whitebeard's sailboat race

Odlaw's treasure hunt

The who-can-catch-the-most-fish race

p. 76 THE TREASURE TRAMPLE
D2

p. 77 NORSE CODE
MAP IN HAND FOR PIRATE GOLD

p. 78 SNAKY SEARCH

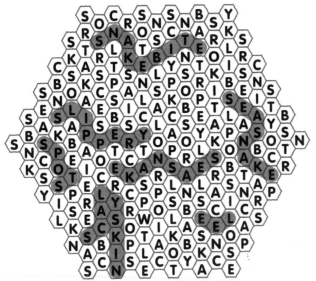

p. 87 FISHING NET SETS

p. 85 MESSAGE IN A BOTTLE

Sand castle; Quicksand; Sunblock; Sunglasses; Pirate ship; Shipwreck; Sea horse; Seashell

p. 90 BLOWING BUBBLES

Mermaid; Seaweed; Turtle; Snorkel; Squid; Yacht; Island; Shark; Reef; Crab; Tide

Copyright © 1987–2016 by Martin Handford

All rights reserved. No part of this book may be reproduced, transmitted, or stored in an information retrieval system in any form or by any means, graphic, electronic, or mechanical, including photocopying, taping, and recording, without prior written permission from the publisher.

First U.S. edition 2016

ISBN 978-0-7636-8811-0

16 17 18 19 20 21 WKT 10 9 8 7 6 5 4 3 2 1

Printed in Shenzhen, Guangdong, China

This book was typeset
in Optima and Wallyfont.
The illustrations were done in ink and
watercolor or in ink and colored digitally.

visit us at www.candlewick.com

ONE LAST THING . . .

You didn't think there'd be a treasure hunt without somewhere to put the precious things, did you? Seek out Waldo's treasure chest (it has a red-and-white striped label)! Also find a bejeweled Woof doghouse!